SOPHIE the DAREDEVIL

Finding the right name isn't easy!
See what else Sophie tries out....

1: SOPHIE the AWESOME

2: SOPHIE the HERO

3: SOPHIE the CHATTERBOX

4: SOPHIE the ZILLIONAIRE

5: SOPHIE the SNOOP

6: SOPHIE the DAREDEVIL

7: SOPHIE the SWEETHEART

SOPHIE the DAREDEVIL

by Lara Bergen

illustrated by Laura Tallardy

SCHOLASTIC INC.

New York   Toronto   London   Auckland
Sydney   Mexico City   New Delhi   Hong Kong

For the daredevil in everyone!

No part of this publication may be reproduced, stored in a retrieval system, or transmitted in any form or by any means, electronic, mechanical, photocopying, recording, or otherwise, without written permission of the publisher. For information regarding permission, write to Scholastic Inc., Attention: Permissions Department, 557 Broadway, New York, NY 10012.

ISBN 978-0-545-26484-6

12 11 10 9 8 7 6 5 4 3   11 12 13 14 15 16/0

Printed in the U.S.A.   40
First printing, July 2011
Designed by Tim Hall

Sophie looked down at the cup in front of her. It was full. Very full. And what it was full of did not look very good.

"Drink it!" said Jack. He leaned across the lunch table.

Sophie sighed and waited for it. . . .

"Go ahead. I *dare* you!"

The other kids from her class were all gathered around. "Drink it! Drink it!" they chanted.

"I will, I will," Sophie said at last. "You dared me. And there's not a dare that I won't do."

But she also couldn't help leaning back in her chair. *Whew!* That cup did not smell very good!

It pretty much smelled like the things that were in it. And by themselves, those things were okay. Sophie liked milk. And fruit punch. And chocolate pudding. And ketchup. And applesauce. And ranch dressing. And chicken noodle soup.

But together?

Not so much.

But Sophie had asked for it. Well . . . she had asked for a *dare*. Anything to help her prove her great new name.

Sophie the Daredevil! How good did that sound?! Sophie had been looking for a name that would make her stand out. She was tired of feeling average in every single way. She was sure the right name could change that. And here it was, at last!

It had come to her when she had put that hat on—the one that Archie Dolan had *licked*.

"I dare you to put it on," he told her.

"Oh, yeah?" she said.

And she did!

No one thought she would do it. (Who knew what kind of germs Archie had?) But Sophie stared Archie in the eyeball and totally showed them.

Of course, as soon as Sophie got the hat home, she washed it really, really well.

Sophie knew if she could do *that* dare, she could do any dare in the world. And she made sure to tell her friends the next day: "Dare me! Bring it on!"

She had lots of ideas about what some extra-fun dares would be. Dares like climbing up the big oak tree. Or jumping off the swing. Or holding her breath for a whole minute. (She even started practicing that one.)

But so far, her friends' dares had been... different. In a word, they had been GROSS.

So far, Sophie had licked the blacktop *and* the school bus window. She had smelled Dean's sneakers (both of them!) and sat on a mysterious wet spot.

Then there was the lunchroom. That was getting to be too much. This "Drink of Doom" was Sophie's second one.

Sophie looked down at the lumpy liquid. A noodle floated to the top.

"Drink it! Drink it! Drink it!" her friends chanted.

She swallowed hard to keep the pizza she'd just eaten from coming up.

Sophie's best friend, Kate, patted her back. "Close your eyes and pretend it's a smoothie. Just like the last time," she said.

"Right." Sophie made a face. She wondered if she'd ever drink a smoothie again. She guessed she would if someone *dared* her. *Ugh.* That thought made her feel worse!

At last, she sat up straight. She took a deep breath and grabbed the cup. She pinched her nose with her other hand and squeezed her eyes shut.

Gulp . . . gulp . . . gulp. She let the liquid slosh down her throat.

Then she put the cup down and covered her mouth. *Uh-oh.* She did not feel good.

For a second she thought, *Was it worth it?*

Then a cheer rang out: "Yay, Sophie!"

She grinned. Yep! It was worth it. She had shown everyone that she was a daredevil *again.*

Plus her friends had to be tired of gross dares now. She turned to Kate, and they high-fived.

That was when Eve slid a plate in front of Sophie. "Hey, Sophie. I dare you to eat *this!*" she said.

Oh, boy.

Sophie looked down. It was a sandwich. She slowly lifted the top piece of bread. Sure enough, it looked like everyone in the lunchroom had added something to it. Though thanks to the chocolate pudding on top, it was kind of hard to tell.

"Eat it! Eat it! Eat it!" Quickly, a new chant started up.

"It's going to be hard to pretend this is a smoothie, isn't it?" Kate said, giggling.

Sophie sighed. She rolled her eyes. Was this the best they could do? Sophie was ready and willing to do *anything*—not only swallow disgusting food.

Where were the "ride your bike with no hands" dares? Or the "knock on mean old Mrs. Corrigan's door" dares? Where were the "skateboard blindfolded" dares? Not that she really wanted one of those.

She crossed her arms. "I am Sophie the *Daredevil*. Not Sophie the Garbage Disposal," she declared. "Doesn't somebody want to dare me to do something just plain *daring*?" she asked.

Eve frowned and looked down at the sandwich. Some other kids shrugged. Some other kids nodded and seemed to try to think of stuff.

Good, Sophie thought. Now maybe her stomach could take a break.

She rubbed her hands together. "Somebody dare me! Go ahead."

"*I* have a dare for you," somebody said.

Sophie turned to see the somebody.

It was Toby Myers!

Uh-oh.

CHAPTER 2

Sophie tried to tell herself not to worry. What was the worst thing Toby could say? But as soon as she thought about *that*, she got even more afraid.

That was the whole problem with Toby—you never knew what you would get. Just when Sophie thought he was the worst boy ever, he'd do something nice. Then when she thought he was maybe okay, he'd do something super-slimy, like give Archie her hat to lick!

And to think that back in first grade he had been her very best friend!

Anyway, that had been a long time ago. Now she tried her best not to think about him. But he had a dare. And Sophie had asked for it.

"Okay," she said. "There's not a dare that I won't do."

Toby grinned. *Double uh-oh,* thought Sophie. That couldn't be good.

Everyone at the lunch table leaned forward.

"I dare you . . . to go into the boys' bathroom!" Toby said.

"Oooh!" The sound rolled around the table. Sophie felt a tingle shoot straight to her toes.

Go into the boys' room! That was a terrible, horrible dare! So terrible and horrible it was by far the best one yet!

Sophie almost wanted to *thank* Toby. But of course, she couldn't do that. Instead, she turned to Kate.

Kate looked as thrilled as Sophie felt. "Are you going to do it?"

"You bet!" Sophie's eyes said.

Then she turned back to Toby. She looked

him square in his beady blue eyes. "I accept your dare," she told him.

"You do?" He looked surprised.

The rest of the class all looked different. Some looked happy. Some did not.

Grace looked worried. "But that's against the rules."

Sydney looked horrified. "Ew! Think of all the germs!"

Jack looked confused. "How will we know if you went in? We can only leave class to go to the bathroom one at a time," he said.

"What? You mean you don't trust me? I am insulted!" Sophie cried. "Remember, I was Sophie the Honest not too long ago!"

"It's not that...," Eve assured her.

"But some proof would be nice," Dean added.

Hmm. Well... Sophie could bring in a camera from home, she guessed.

But Toby had another idea. "How about I go in first? I'll write a note on toilet paper, and you'll have to bring it back."

Archie slapped him on the shoulder. "I like it!" he said. "That means she has to go into the *stall!* Ha!" He laughed.

Ugh! Sophie's tingles felt pricklier. She squirmed to shake them down. She was up for popping into the boys' room. And for popping right back out. But a whole tour of the place? That was a lot. . . .

"What's wrong, Sophster?" Toby asked. "Are you chickening out?"

Archie flapped his elbows. "Bwock! Bwock! Bwock!" he squawked.

But Kate put her arm around Sophie. "Oh, shut your beak, Archie. Sophie's not chickening out."

Right, thought Sophie. She would never chicken out! After all, dares weren't supposed to be easy. They were supposed to give you tingles. That's what doing them was all about.

Sophie crossed her arms and shot Toby her most daring "I'll show *you!*" glare.

Just then, their teacher, Ms. Moffly, walked up.

"Clean your trays," she told the class.

Then she stopped by Sophie's place and looked down at the sandwich Eve had made. "Is that your lunch, Sophie M.?" she asked.

Sophie shrugged. "It's more like *everyone's* lunch," she said.

☆   ☆   ☆

Like any true daredevil, Sophie couldn't wait to do Toby's dare!

But she had to wait for Toby to go to the boys' room first and leave the note. And almost an hour passed before he did that.

First, at recess after lunch, he *had* to play basketball. Of course.

Then, back in the classroom, he *had* to wait for Mia's birthday cupcakes to be served.

Sure, Sophie liked cupcakes, too. And classroom birthdays were always fun (even though they reminded her that *her* birthday — June 30 — never got a real one). It was just that, for the first time, Sophie wished her friend's birthday was some other day. A day when her mind wasn't full of dares, and her stomach wasn't full of Drink of Doom.

Sophie watched Mia pass out her cupcakes. "Hurry up," she almost said. Why did Mia have to be so careful? In a few minutes, they'd be eaten all up, anyway.

Sophie took hers. It was vanilla, in a shiny foil cup. She wished that it were chocolate. But she knew why it was not. Ben was allergic to chocolate, and he was Mia's best friend in the whole world.

Sophie wondered if Mia might change her mind now that she was eight. Ben was fun to play with. And he had a real air hockey table, too. But between the chocolate thing *and* the being-a-boy thing...Well, that was a lot to overlook.

When everyone had a cupcake, it was time to sing the birthday song. Ms. Moffly got it started, and soon the whole class was singing along. Well, most of the class was singing. Toby and Archie were barking like dogs. And Sophie's mouth was just moving. There wasn't much

sound. Sometimes when she sang, she made funny noises, so she tried not to let too many out.

At last, the celebration was over — even the *"Are you one! Are you two! . . ."* part.

Sophie looked across the room at Toby. Was he finally ready to go?

No. He had chewed up his cupcake wrapper into a little spitty ball. Now he was showing it to Archie. Gross!

What are you waiting for, Toby? Sophie wondered. *Go to the bathroom already! Please!*

Just then, Toby raised his hand. "Ms. Moffly, can I go to the boys' room?" he asked.

Yes! Sophie's heart beat faster.

Ms. Moffly nodded. "Of course, Toby," she said. "But try not to take as long as you sometimes do. We're going to begin our unit on fractions, and I'd hate for you to miss a *fraction* of it!"

Sophie and the rest of the class watched Toby get up and go. He waved as he walked out. He didn't look at Sophie, though.

"Okay," said Ms. Moffly. "Let's start by talking about *half*." Of course, since only *half* of Sophie was paying attention, she wasn't 100 percent sure that was what Ms. Moffly said.

The rest of her was thinking about Toby, and about how she couldn't wait for him to get back. It was hard to sit there calmly and listen while inside she was all fizzed up.

Did every daredevil feel this way? Probably so. Sophie guessed she would have to get used to feeling that way from now on.

It seemed to take forever. Ms. Moffly finished halves and went on to fourths.

Then, finally, the door creaked open. Toby walked in. He looked straight at her.

Sophie took a deep breath. She raised her hand. High.

At last! It was her turn!

CHAPTER 3

BOYS.

Sophie had seen the sign a zillion times. Maybe more. But she had never seen it this way. So big. Right in front of her nose.

"Come in. I dare you," it seemed to say. This was the first time a door had talked to her.

Sophie looked up at it. "Oh, yeah?" she said back. "Go ahead and dare me. I'm Sophie the Daredevil, you know!"

Then she quickly looked around. She had to make sure she was alone. She was very happy to *do* the dare. But getting in trouble for it? Not so much.

The hall was empty. The coast was all clear. Sophie took a deep breath, reached for the handle...

...and jumped back as the door swung out!

A tall boy looked down at her.

Oh, no!

Sophie froze. It was Sam, a fifth grader. He was in the same class as her big sister, Hayley. Hayley had even *liked* him for a week. He was also Dean's big brother. They had the same big head and bright pink cheeks.

It took him a second to recognize Sophie. But she could tell as soon as he did.

"Aren't you in third grade?" he asked. She nodded, and he pointed to the sign on the bathroom door. "Then you should know how to read."

"Oops." Sophie shrugged and tried very hard not to say, "I do."

Sam walked away. She heard him mutter, "I can't wait till I get to middle school."

Me too! she thought as he turned the corner. What had Hayley seen in him?

Then more thoughts suddenly hit her. Thoughts like: *Phew! That was close.*

And: *What if another boy is still in the bathroom?*

Sophie guessed she should wait outside to see. So she did.

She counted to three. Then she reached for the door again. And this time, she slipped in.

Sophie held her breath as she looked around. Then she let it out. She was alone!

So. This was the boys' room. She let her eyes take it in.

There were two sinks. And two stalls. And that was about it.

Oh. There were also two mirrors. *Well, that's a waste*, Sophie thought.

Basically, the boys' bathroom looked a lot like the girls'. It was weird.

But *something* had to be different. . . .

Sophie sniffed. Oh! The smell. *That* was it.

Well, there was no reason for Sophie to hang out there for too long. It was time to find Toby's note. So she checked the first stall.

Crreeeak.

Sophie froze.

Help!!! she thought.

Somebody else had come into the bathroom. She wasn't alone!

Sophie didn't know what to do. And she didn't stop to think. Her hand flew out all by itself and closed the stall door. *BANG!*

Then she looked down. Her shoes were sneakers. That was okay. But her socks? They were rainbow striped and polka-dotted. Would a boy ever wear those? No way!

She should have jumped up onto the toilet seat. But she guessed it was too late.

So she just stood there, very, very still. She held her breath and waited for the boy to finish up and go.

Then she suddenly heard humming. Sophie

was sure she knew that tune. She listened even harder? Was it the ABC song? *Hmm . . .*

Sophie couldn't help it: She had to see who the boy was. She put her eye to the space between the stall and the door.

What?

It wasn't a boy! It was the grown-up principal!

He was washing his hands at the sink. *Okay, don't panic*, Sophie told herself. But what if he saw her? And she had to go to his office? That would be two trips to the principal's office . . . that week!

At last, she heard the water turn off. The hand dryer came on with a *whrrrrr!* The ABC humming stopped. And — *crrreak* — Principal Tate opened the door.

He had just come in to wash his hands! *Phew!* Sophie let out her breath.

Now that's what being a daredevil's all about! she told herself.

She couldn't wait to get back and tell Kate. And everyone else!

But—*oh, right*—she still had to find Toby's note. She reached for the toilet paper and pulled. But there wasn't any note on it. And there wasn't any note in the next stall.

Had Toby forgotten?

Or was he trying to play some dirty trick?

Or maybe Sam had *used* the toilet paper. *Ew.* Sophie guessed that could be it.

It didn't matter, really. What mattered was that she had nothing to show. She had nothing to prove that she had done the dare!

Sophie was so mad she stomped her foot.

That was when she saw it: a piece of toilet paper on the floor. Were there words on it? Yes!

Sophie bent down to read what they were.

I dare you to pick this up.

Yuck! The paper was wet!

Sophie sighed. She should have known that Toby would make this an extra-hard dare.

Is touching it worth it? she asked herself. *Of course it is!*

After all, she was Sophie the Daredevil! The harder the dare, the better! Right?

She stuck out her tongue and picked up the paper with two fingers. Then she hurried to the door. But at the very same time, a kindergartner walked in. He looked up at her and the sign on the door.

"If you're wondering, I *can* read," she said, running past him. "I'm just a daredevil. Get used to it!"

CHAPTER 4

Sophie had some explaining to do when she got back to room 10.

"What took you so long?" Ms. Moffly asked.

Sophie could feel a huge smile busting out. She bit her lip to keep it in.

"I'm sorry. I tried to be fast," she said. It was the truth. Wasn't it?

Ms. Moffly shook her head and turned back to the board. Sophie held up the toilet paper and the other kids cheered.

"I didn't know you were all such big fans of fractions," Ms. Moffly said, spinning back around. "But let's hold our applause until the end. Okay, class?"

Sophie giggled and went back to her seat. She shared a table with Kate and Sydney and Grace. As Ms. Moffly started writing out fractions again, Sophie laid the soggy toilet paper square out for them to see.

"There really isn't a dare you won't do, is there?" Kate said, patting her back.

Grace shook her head. "I wouldn't have done it. That's for sure."

"You have to tell us everything," Sydney whispered, leaning in.

And Sophie did, when it was free time. That was Sophie's favorite part of the day. That's when they got to start their homework, or read, or play games. Today, of course, it was the time for Sophie to tell everyone everything.

"I can't believe you did it!" Eve said.

"I can't believe you didn't get caught," said Grace.

"That's the best part!" Sophie told them. "I almost did! Isn't that great?"

She told them about how Sam had seen her. And how Principal Tate had come in. "And guess what," she added. "He hums the ABC song while he washes his hands!"

A few of the kids laughed. Sophie's grin got very big.

"So tell us about the boys' room!" Kate urged. "What was it like?"

"Well . . ." *There's not much to say about it, really*, Sophie thought. "It's kind of just a bathroom, like ours," she began.

But she could see that the girls were disappointed. So she decided to say a little more.

"But our bathroom is *so* much better in *so* many ways," she went on.

"Yes!" The girls pumped their fists.

All the boys frowned.

Still, even the boys were impressed by her amazing, *daring* feat — Toby and Archie included. Sophie could tell. And it felt great!

Ben even said, "Sophie, you really are a daredevil!"

There was only one person who did not seem to care. And that person was Mindy VonBoffmann, the snootiest girl in room 10.

Of course, none of Sophie's great names had impressed Mindy before. So why should this one be different? Sophie wasn't sure.

Maybe it was because she had been *so* daring this time. After all, no other girl had ever gone in the boys' room before.

Or maybe it was because she was just tired of being ignored. She wanted her name to be one that *everyone* called her.

So a little later, back at their table, Sophie talked about it with Kate.

"I don't get it," Sophie said. "I've done six different dares today. And Mindy hasn't said a thing."

Kate shrugged. "You know Mindy. If it's not about her, she doesn't care. Now, if your name was Sophie the *Mindy*, she'd be into that, I bet!"

She grinned. It was a joke. But it was kind of true, too.

Sophie sighed. "Yeah, I guess. But I still wish Mindy thought I was a daredevil. Hey!" She felt a great idea pop into her head. "Should I ask *her* to dare me? What do you think of that?"

Kate put down her pencil. (They were supposed to be writing answers—in complete sentences— to social studies questions right then.) She turned to face Sophie. "I think that would be a really big mistake," she said.

"Yeah, probably." Sophie nodded.

Besides, who cared what Mindy thought?

Oh... Sophie couldn't help it. *She* did. A lot.

After the bell rang at the end of the day, Sophie walked up to Mindy. "So, Mindy," she said.

Mindy was zipping her jacket. It had a furry collar and cuffs. She fluffed her hair and looked at Sophie. "So what?"

Mindy's best friend, Lily Lemley, stood beside her. Lily fluffed *her* hair, too. "Yeah, so what?" she said, like there was an echo in the room.

Mindy looked down her nose. "We still don't want to see your toilet paper, Sophie, if that's what you're wondering," she said.

"Oh, no." Sophie slid the toilet paper into her pocket and shook her head. "I was just wondering, since I am a daredevil, if *you* had a dare for me."

Mindy frowned a pinchy frown. It almost looked like she was mad. But then something happened. Half her frown turned upside down.

Sophie held her breath and waited. Mindy was thinking; Sophie could tell. She bet she was thinking of something Mindyish. Something like, oh, kissing her shoe. But if that was what it took to make Mindy think she was a daredevil, then that was exactly what Sophie would do.

Bring it on, Sophie thought.

But Mindy did not.

Instead, she said, "Let me think about it. Here. Take my backpack, Lily. Let's go."

Hmph!

CHAPTER 5

The next day was Saturday. *Yay!* That meant a bunch of great things:

No school.

TV in the morning.

And chocolate chip pancakes!

Plus this Saturday there was one more great thing: Mia's birthday party. *Hooray!*

Well, it was a *half*-great thing, really. The great part was that the party was at the brand-new rec center pool. But *boys* were invited, which made it half horrible, too.

None of the girls had been happy when Mia

told them that news. At first, Sydney even said she wasn't going. Boys ruined everything, according to her.

Mia told them she couldn't help it. She said her mom had made her invite the whole class. But Sophie knew the real reason the boys were invited: Mia had to invite Ben because he was her best friend. And parents seemed to have this rule that when you invited one boy or girl, you had to invite all of them.

Sophie thought that was another good reason not to have a boy for a best friend.

Oh, well. No party was perfect. And Mia said it was a very big pool. Maybe there was even a *baby* pool for the boys to use. (Ha! Kate had told her that joke. Sophie thought it was pretty good.)

Still, Sophie could hardly wait for the party. She dug out her bathing suit as soon as she got up in the morning. The party didn't start until two. But she put it on, anyway.

The suit was Sophie's favorite—a blue-green

tankini with lots and lots of butterflies. But . . . *Hmmm.* Sophie guessed she had grown since the summer. She didn't remember it feeling so tight.

And look. . . . There was her belly button. She didn't think that had showed before.

No, her suit didn't look—or feel—as good as it used to. But that was okay. At least it matched her hair that day!

"Your *hair*!" her mom had exclaimed as soon as she'd seen it the night before.

That was pretty much what her dad had said, too. But he added, "Is it real?!"

Yes, it was real. Real hair—that was really *blue*!

Why? Because her sister, Hayley, had said, "I dare you."

Sophie had asked her for a dare. And Hayley had blue hair spray left from last Halloween.

"I dare you to do it. And wear it all weekend," said Hayley.

So of course Sophie did!

She really liked it, too. It looked super-daring, just like a daredevil's hair should!

Sure enough, when Sophie got to the rec center, her hair got oohs and aahs right away.

"Too bad you have to wear a swim cap!" Kate said.

Yes, it was too bad. But what could she do? Sophie could dare to break the swim cap rule, but she'd just get kicked out of the pool.

She put on her white rubber swim cap. (*Ugh.* It was even tighter than her suit.) Then she grabbed Kate's hand, and they followed Grace and Sydney to the pool.

It really was big! And it was indoors, which was so cool!

The only other indoor pool Sophie had been to was in a hotel she had stayed in last spring break. That was definitely the best part of her family trip to Washington, D.C. But that pool seemed like a puddle now. This pool was a million times bigger, at least!

Sophie walked—she didn't run—to the ed
(That was a pool rule, she knew.) Some of
her friends were already swimming. Sophie
couldn't wait to jump in, too!

But just then, Mia and Eve and Ben walked up.

"Yay! You're here!" said Mia. "Want to try the
slide with us?"

Slide? Sophie turned. *Wow!* Talk about cool!
There was a real waterslide. And it was swirly,
too! But that wasn't all. There was something
else at the end of the pool. Not one, but *two*
diving boards. And one of them was super
high!

Sophie crossed her arms. She knew something right then for sure. No matter how many
boys came, this would be the best party in the
world! Why? Because there were *millions* of
dares to do in this pool!

Dares like holding her breath underwater.
And going down the slide headfirst. And what
about the high dive? Who would dare her to
jump from that?

ldn't wait to find out. And she

staring at the high dive. "Hey, Sophie. What would you do if I dared you to jump from there?"

Sophie put her hands on her hips. "I'd do it. Of course!" she said.

"Whoa!" Ben looked surprised.

Kate made a "really?" face. "Are you sure? It's pretty high, you know."

Sophie stuck out her chin. "You know there's not a dare that I won't do! That high dive has my name all over it!"

"Hey, everyone!" Mia shouted. Most of the class was now in the pool. "Guess what. I dared Sophie to jump off the high dive. And she's going to!"

"Wow!"

"Ooh!"

Sophie grinned and took it all in. She felt like she'd been wrapped up in a warm towel. She took a quick bow. Then she walked—she didn't run—across the deck to the diving boards.

She reached the ladder and bowed again. She heard a few more whoops and cheers.

Then she heard a whistle. "Hey, you! Not so fast!"

Huh? Sophie looked over her shoulder. A lifeguard was staring at Sophie from her chair.

"How old are you?" the guard asked.

"Um . . . eight." Couldn't she tell?

"Well, if you're under twelve, you have to pass a high-dive test," the lifeguard said.

Then she pointed to a sign. It said pretty much the same thing.

"Oh . . ." A test? *Really?* thought Sophie. "So . . . what does that mean?"

The lifeguard explained that it meant she had to swim the *looong* way across the pool. Then she had to tread water. In the deep end. For a whole minute.

But that was no problem! "I can do that!" Sophie said.

She had done exactly the same thing in the old, outdoor rec pool. She had never liked taking swim lessons very much. But now she was glad her mom forced her to.

She jumped in and started swimming... and treading water... until she passed the test. Then she climbed out of the deep end. *Whew.*

"I did it!" Sophie called.

"The diving board's all yours," the lifeguard replied. Then she leaned out of her chair. "Hey, kid! You're *blue*! Are you alright?"

Blue? What was she talking about? Sophie looked down. Sure enough, a bright blue puddle was forming below her on the tile.

Oh, no! What's wrong with me? Sophie worried. But a second later, she knew. It was Hayley's blue hair spray. It had washed off in the pool!

Hayley had never said if it was waterproof. And Sophie had never thought to ask. Now she didn't have to.

She wiped her face off with her hands. Yep. They were blue, too.

The lifeguard pointed to the locker room. "I think you need a shower," she said, "before you get back in this pool."

☆   ☆   ☆

Sophie came back from the shower clean and ready to jump. But there was one big problem. No one was watching anymore. Now everyone was playing Marco Polo in the shallow end.

Sophie waved. But nobody saw her. "Yoo-hoo!" She waved again.

At last, Kate noticed her. "Hey!" she yelled. "Sophie's back! She's going to try again!"

Sophie grinned and waved "thanks" to Kate. Then she took another bow. Then she grabbed the ladder and started climbing. One rung...two rungs...until she started slowing down.

Wow. This diving board really *was* high!

How high had she climbed?

She stopped to look down.

Agh! She was way, WAY off the ground.

Sophie quickly looked back up. The top was still far away. A lump was lumping in her throat. She tried to swallow it. But it stayed.

"Go, Sophie!" she heard kids shout. And suddenly, she wished she were down with them, splashing and playing in the shallow end.

Then she stopped. What was she thinking? If she were *there*, who would she be? She sure wouldn't be Sophie the Daredevil anymore. She wouldn't be special. And she wouldn't be unique.

She swallowed her lump (or at least most of it). And she started to climb again.

"Go, Sophie, go!" she heard. And it helped a little bit. Still, Sophie couldn't help shaking. She wondered if everyone could tell. And would her trembling, slippery hands hold her? She was almost surprised that they did.

Finally, she got to the top.

"Yay!" the kids in the pool below cheered.

Yay . . . and HELP! Sophie thought.

She closed her eyes and reminded herself, *I am a daredevil! There's not a dare I won't do. I've already worn a hat that Archie licked. And I stuck my nose in Dean's shoes. (Ew!) I've even been in the boys' bathroom. And dyed my hair blue! Dares aren't supposed to be easy. They're supposed to be hard. And they're supposed to give you tingles. Even if the tingles don't feel good.*

Okay. That seemed to work. A little. She could do this. She could. She just had to open her eyes and step forward. So she did. . . .

AHHHH!

She stepped back as fast as she could.

What was she thinking? She could not look over the edge. She was at least a mile high. She needed a parachute for this!

Meanwhile, her friends were waving. They looked far away . . . and small. And the water below her? It looked far away . . . and hard.

I have to jump. And I will! Sophie thought.

Just as soon as I count to ten. One . . . two . . . three . . .

She got to ten. And didn't move.

She still wasn't ready. So she tried it again...
but it still didn't work.

Maybe if she counted backward?

Ten...nine...eight...

Her mind was saying, "Jump, Sophie the
Daredevil! If you can go in the boys' room, you
can jump in a pool!" But it didn't matter. The
rest of her was saying, "Don't move!"

Meanwhile, a brand-new handstand contest
had started in the shallow end. Everyone had
gotten tired of waiting—except for Kate. She put
her hands up as if to say, "What gives?"

"Hey, kid," the lifeguard called. Sophie was
way above her now. "You've got to jump, you
know. If you can't, you've got to climb down.
Those are the rules."

Sophie bit her lip. Climb down? Would Sophie
the Daredevil really climb down?

Now she didn't know which was worse: risking
her life by jumping, or risking her name by
giving up!

CHAPTER 6

"*B*wock! Bwock! Look! It's Sophie the Chicken! So there *is* a dare she can't do!"

Sophie's eyes zoomed around and landed on Toby and Archie. *Grrrrr!* Her hands made fists.

Archie was pointing and laughing. But Toby was doing something worse: He was flapping his bony elbows and totally making fun of her!

Sophie stopped trembling. Completely. *Sophie the Chicken, huh?!* She put her hands on her hips. "I am not a chicken, either!" she called. She took a step forward. "I am a—*AGGHHHH!!!*"

Oh, no! What had she done?

Had she stepped off the edge of the board? She hadn't meant to step that far!

Sophie's eyes were shut tight . . . but yes, she was pretty sure that was what she had done.

She was falling through the air. Her arms flapped, but they could not keep her up. At least she wasn't screaming — now that her stomach was in her throat.

Sophie wondered how long it would last. How long did it take to fall a whole mile? Should she try to open her eyes? Should she try to hold her nose? Should she try to stop waving her arms and legs before she —

Smack!

— hit the water?

Ouch!

Sophie opened her eyes then. She was underwater. Way under, in fact. She pulled and kicked until she popped to the surface. She gulped for air. *Hooray!* She was still alive.

And then it suddenly hit her: She had done the dare! She was *still*, without a doubt, for sure, the most daring kid in her whole class!

Sophie beamed as she climbed out of the deep end.

Kate was there to meet her. "Are you okay?"

Sophie nodded. "Of course! I'm awesome! *So?* How was my jump?" she asked.

Kate's mouth twisted. Her nose wrinkled. "It looked like it hurt," she said.

Sophie pumped her fist. "Yes!" she said. "That makes it even *more* daring! Doesn't it?"

She stood up, dripping, and fixed her bathing suit. (The jump had — *oops* — twisted it some.)

"I sure showed Toby and Archie, didn't I!" she told Kate.

"Um...yeah...," Kate said. But she didn't look so sure.

Sophie turned to bow to the shallow end, just like any great daredevil should.

"Yeah!"

"Yay!"

Wow! Were those cheers?

"Listen to that!" she said to Kate.

But Kate did not look thrilled. Instead, she pointed up. Sophie followed her finger. The next second, her jaw dropped.

Toby was standing up on the high dive! He did a strong-man pose. Then he yelled, *"Ay, caramba!"* and ran . . . and jumped!

Sophie couldn't believe it.

He didn't!

But he did.

Kate put her hand on Sophie's shoulder. "Who cares? You were the first," she said.

Right. Sophie nodded. That was the truth. Anyone could go *second*. Daredevils went *first*.

Plus Toby's jump didn't even look like it hurt!

Still, it was Toby who had gotten those cheers. And that wasn't fair. It was giving Sophie a feeling. The feeling of losing her name. There was only one thing to do, she knew: climb back up and jump again.

And this time, she should do it backward. Or maybe add a flip.

But what if she climbed back up and was afraid to jump again?

She looked at the diving board high above her. Yeah. That could happen, she guessed.

Plus she really wanted to slide down the water-slide and do handstands in the shallow end.

Being a daredevil was so hard! Sophie sighed. She had to choose. Then she sighed again. Nope, she didn't have to choose—because Mia's mom was calling them.

"Time to get out of the pool, kids! There's pizza and cake in the party room!"

Great, Sophie thought. This should have been the best party ever. Now it was the worst. And all because of Toby. Mia should never have invited boys!

☆　　☆　　☆

The girls went to their locker room, while the boys all went to theirs. The girls showered and changed out of their bathing suits.

"That was so much fun!" Sydney said.

"I'm totally having my birthday party here, too!" Grace declared.

"I kind of wish I'd tried the high dive.... Hey, did you ever do it, Sophie?" Mia asked.

What?

"Yes! Didn't you see me? You're the one who dared me!" Sophie said.

Mia shrugged. "Sorry. I started to watch. But you took so long, I gave up, I guess."

No!

"Yeah," said Sophie A. (She was the other Sophie in Sophie's class.) "I thought you changed your mind. I thought you were going to climb down."

Sophie frowned. How could she say that? (And how could she tell that climbing down was exactly what had been in Sophie's mind?)

"But you dared me," Sophie argued. "And there's never been a dare I wouldn't do."

"Sorry," Mia told her. "That's right. I almost forgot."

Almost forgot?

Sophie looked around. "Didn't *anybody* see me jump?"

Kate waved. "I did."

"So did I," Sydney said.

Phew.

Then Sydney went on. "But I thought you fell in. Did it hurt?"

"Uh . . . yes. A little." Sophie nodded. "That was the extra-daring part."

Then Eve spoke up. "I did see Toby jump!"

"Yeah, me too," said Sophie A.

"He was so funny." Mia laughed.

Sophie couldn't help it. *Grrrrr!* Her hands balled into fists again.

"You know he only did it because I dared to do it first," she said.

"Totally." Kate nodded.

"Yeah." A few other girls did, too.

"You're probably right," Mia said. "Hey, I'm starving. Let's go to the party room!"

All the girls followed her, even Sophie.

But Sophie was slow. She was mad at Toby for spoiling her dare. But she was worried, too. She hoped her friends weren't starting to think that she wasn't much of a daredevil after all. At the same time, deep inside, she was starting to think it might be true.

She *might* have climbed down from the high dive if she hadn't fallen in.

But Sophie the Daredevil was such a perfect name ... or it had been.

By the time Sophie got to the party room, she knew what she needed to do. She had to prove that she was a real daredevil. That she was brave enough to do any dare, no matter what. And that was why—for the first time ever—Sophie was happy when Mindy walked up.

"Remember when you asked me for a dare, Sophie?" Mindy smiled. "Well, if you really think you're so daring, I have one for you."

CHAPTER 7

Mindy had a dare? This was perfect!

"Bring it on!" Sophie said.

"Shhh," Mindy told her. "Not so loud." She looked around.

Sophie's shoulders sank. "Hang on. The dare isn't that I have to go into the boys' locker room, is it?" she asked.

Mindy slowly grinned. "Oh, don't worry. It's nothing like that."

"Good," Sophie said. Then she noticed something odd. "Hey, where's Lily?"

"I left my mermaid towel by the pool. So she went back to get it." Mindy shrugged.

Sophie rolled her eyes. How did Mindy get Lily to do things like that?

She leaned in toward Mindy. "So what is your dare?"

Mindy wrapped some hair around her finger. Her eyes cut away. Sophie turned to see what Mindy was looking at. The present table?

"I dare you to take one of Mia's gifts from there," Mindy said in a low voice.

Sophie didn't get it. "Why?"

"Because I dare you." Mindy's eyes narrowed. "Or are you afraid?"

Afraid? Sophie the Daredevil? Of course she was not! She just thought taking other people's presents was kind of . . . stealing. And that it was kind of . . . wrong.

But what if Sophie took her own gift? It wasn't *really* Mia's yet, after all. Then Sophie could give it to Mia later, like she'd meant to do that all along.

"Well?" Mindy said. She let go of her hair and it bounced up.

Sophie crossed her arms and nodded. "Okay. Consider it done." Then she turned toward the other table, where everyone was sitting down for lunch.

"Hang on," said Mindy quickly. "I didn't tell you which one."

Oh. Sophie turned back. So Mindy had a special present in mind. . . .

Mindy nodded to one with shiny silver paper. "I dare you to take that one, with the purple bow."

That purple-bow gift was Kate's. Sophie had seen her carry it in.

"Okay?" Mindy's grin looked just a little mean. "Is it still a deal?"

"I said I'd do your dare," Sophie told her. "And I will."

She didn't want to—at all. But what else could a daredevil do? Besides, Sophie only had to *take* the present. She didn't have to *keep* it. Right?

She'd take it and show Mindy. And right away, she'd put it back.

But first it was time to eat. Mia's parents were passing out the pizza. And Kate was waving to Sophie and calling, "Over here! I saved you a place."

Sophie waved back and hurried over. She slipped into a seat between Sydney and Kate.

"So what was Mindy talking to you about?" Kate asked.

"Uh...," Sophie mumbled. She really didn't want to say.

She wasn't surprised that Kate had asked. Mindy hardly ever talked to them. And Sophie always told Kate everything. After all, Kate was her best friend. Still, there was something about Mindy's dare that made her want to keep it in.

"Hmmm?" Kate was waiting for Sophie's answer.

Sophie looked at her pizza instead.

"Hey, look!" she said finally. "The plates all

look like different kinds of balls." She pointed to Kate's soccer ball plate. "Want to trade?"

"No, thanks." Kate grinned and shook her head. "You can keep your football plate. You know I like soccer more! Hey, did you know Mia was going to have a sports theme?"

"I didn't," said Sydney. "As if inviting boys wasn't bad enough!"

They laughed, and Sophie sighed. The subject had been changed! She picked up her pizza and took a bite.

"So . . . what about Mindy?" Kate asked again. *Ugh.*

Sophie chewed as slowly as she could. Then she spotted Mia's mom with the birthday cake. She pointed. "Look!"

Kate turned to see a bright orange mound on a silver tray.

Sydney leaned over. "Is that supposed to be a *ball* cake?"

"Well, I guess it could be a basketball," Sophie said with a shrug.

Kate nodded. "Or maybe Mia's having a space theme, too, and it's the sun."

They watched Mia's mom light the candles. After that, Mia's dad cut the lights. Then the birthday song started. Sophie quietly moved her mouth, as usual, so no funny sounds came out. If only she could have stopped the sounds from Toby's and Archie's mouths, too. They squawked like chickens this time. Sophie couldn't wait for the song to be done.

Mia blew out the candles, and her mom cut the cake. This was usually when people called out for a special piece — like a corner, or a flower, or a piece with the name on it. But it was pretty quiet, since this cake didn't have those things.

Sophie looked down at the piece she got. It was on a baseball plate. But before she took a bite, her eyes and Mindy's met.

"So what are you waiting for?" Mindy's eyes asked.

"Good question," Sophie's said back.

She took a lick of icing. *Mmm.* Butterscotch. Then she pushed her chair back, took a deep breath, and stood up.

"Where are you going?" Kate asked.

"Uh . . . to the bathroom," Sophie said.

Kate nodded to Sophie's plate. "Aren't you going to finish that?" she asked.

Sophie slid her piece of cake toward Kate. "No, you can have it." She grinned. Then she walked toward the gift table, making a plan as she did.

Kate's gift was still on the table, between Sophie's tote bag and the door. All Sophie had to do was get her bag, walk by the table, and let the gift fall in. Then she'd walk out and into the bathroom.

A few minutes later, she'd return. She'd put the gift back on the table. And the dare would be done.

Sophie picked up her tote bag and walked slowly past the gifts. She got to the silver present, held her tote open and nudged it in.

Yes! She'd done it! But had Mindy seen? Sophie quickly checked. Oh, yeah! Mindy's eyes were locked on her. She'd definitely seen.

Nobody else was watching. *Phew!* Not even Kate. She was way too busy licking Sophie's baseball plate. And Mia's parents were busy taking pictures. It was all going just great!

Well, all except one thing: Sophie's heart was beating pretty fast. She even felt a little sweaty. She hadn't planned on that.

So she hurried to the bathroom. She hoped she'd feel better when she got there. And she did, a little. Until she peeked into her bag. Then her heart started to thump. Like on the high dive, only worse!

She knew she'd had to take Mia's gift. Mindy had dared her, and daredevils had to do things they didn't want to sometimes . . . right? Right!

Still, it felt really weird. It didn't feel right at all. Where were all those daring tingles? Why wasn't this dare fun?

She needed to get that gift back on the table

as fast as she could. She washed her hands and her face with cold water and headed back to the party room.

She got to the door and reached for the doorknob of the party room. But before she could turn it, the door opened in. Mia's mom smiled down at her. "Oh, Sophie!" she said. "There you are!" She held out a goody bag. "I hope you had fun." Then she called over her shoulder, "Mia, come thank your guests as they go!"

Hold on. The party was *over*?

Sophie peered into the room and saw the kids gathering their stuff. Mia's dad was by the gift table . . . packing all the presents up.

How could she put Kate's gift back now?

The answer was: She could not!

CHAPTER 8

"Here, let me carry your tote bag for you," Sophie's dad said as they walked out to the car.

"No!" Sophie said quickly. "I've got it!" She held her bag close.

As Sophie walked across the rec center parking lot, her legs felt heavy and slow. At the same time, she couldn't wait to get home.

Ugh! A big part of Sophie wished she'd just put the gift back. But how could she have done that? In front of everyone? There was no way. Sophie was a daredevil. But she was not crazy.

She had thought keeping the gift would be easier, so it was still in her bag. But maybe she had thought wrong.

"So how was the party?" her dad asked. "How was the new pool? And did I hear something about a high dive? That must be pretty cool!"

Sophie shrugged. "It was fine," she said. She knew her dad was waiting for her to go on. But she couldn't. It was like her words were stuck in her tote bag with Mia's gift, deep under her towel.

"What's in the goody bag?" her dad asked as they got to the car. He nodded toward the sack in her other hand. "Any good loot?"

Goody bag? Oh, yeah. Sophie had almost forgotten about that.

She shrugged again and said, "Don't know. I'll look when I get home."

"Really?" Her dad's eyebrows went crooked. "That's not like the Sophie Miller I know."

He opened the car door for Sophie. "Is something wrong?" he asked. "I hope it's not your hair. Looks like all that blue stuff washed out."

"No." Sophie shook her head. That wasn't it at all. She kept her eyes down as she fastened her seat belt. "I'm just ready to go home."

Getting home wouldn't fix things. But at least at home she could hide that dumb present somewhere . . . until she figured out what to do next.

That was why what her dad said then almost made her groan.

"Well, guess what. I have a whole list of errands I have to do. And I thought we could do them together. A little Sophie-and-Daddy time, finally! Won't that be fun?"

He gave her a huge smile. Sophie knew he was waiting for an extra-large "Yes!" So she tried to give him one. But it came out more like a medium "Yeah."

Her dad went on. "I need to get a haircut, and I know how you love going with me to do that. And then I thought we could go to the library to take back some books, and the post office. Then some ice cream. Unless you're too full of cake, of course!" He laughed at that.

Then he climbed into the driver's seat and started the car. At the same time, Sophie slunk down in her own seat as far as she could go.

She let her tote bag slide to the floor. She tried to cover it with her feet. But she could almost hear the present in it taunting her: "You never should have taken me!"

"But I had to," Sophie wanted to tell it. "It wasn't my idea. It was a dare!"

Still, something told her that the present didn't care.

☆　　☆　　☆

Sophie's dad was right. She did love going with him to the barbershop—most of the time.

Most of the time she liked seeing the barbers, Mr. Charlie and Mr. Luis. They gave her lollipops and let her twirl around in their barber chairs. Sometimes they even gave her a broom so she could sweep up hair!

68

But today all Sophie could think was, *There are way too many mirrors in this place!*

Everywhere she looked, she saw a mirror. And in every mirror, she saw herself. And that would have been just fine . . . if it had been a *daring* self.

But it wasn't daring. It was guilty. Guilty and sad and quiet and worried and even almost scared.

"So? How do I look?" Sophie's dad asked her, as always, when Mr. Charlie was done.

"Great, Dad," she told him, as always (even though his hair always looked the same to her).

And as always, Mr. Charlie took a mug of lollipops down off his shelf.

As always, he held it out to her. "Take as many as you want!" he said.

But for the first time, Sophie kept her hand down. For some reason, it didn't seem right. Treats were for girls who deserved them. And Sophie wasn't sure that she did.

Mr. Charlie turned to the other barber. "Who is this shy girl, Luis?" he asked.

Mr. Luis, who was shorter and rounder, held up his short, round hands. "It can't be our Sophie, Charlie," he told him. "She hasn't even asked to sweep!"

Who was she? Good question. Sophie was starting to wonder the same thing. She had thought she was Sophie the Daredevil. But now that didn't seem like quite the right name.

Right now, she felt a lot more like Sophie the Girl with Mia's Gift in Her Bag in the Car.

Or Sophie the Girl Who Didn't Know How to Give It Back to Her.

Or maybe just plain old Sophie the Miserable.

And the nicer anyone was to her, the more miserable she felt!

Still, Sophie didn't want to be rude. So she picked out a brown lollipop. *Yuck.* Root beer, her least favorite flavor. She guessed she deserved *that.*

Next Sophie and her dad walked to the library. Most of the time, Sophie loved going there, too. No matter how many books she took home to read, she could always go back and find something new.

But today the library was also different. Today every book she found made her feel worse!

The Birthday Bandit

A Daring Disaster

I've Got a Secret

Growing Pains

(This last book didn't remind her about Mia's present, actually. It reminded her that her bathing suit was tight and she needed a new one ASAP.)

And then, down at the post office, what did she see? "Wanted" posters, that's what!

Sophie looked at the wall of criminals and suddenly thought, *That could be me!*

And she was still thinking that later, as she and her dad walked down the street.

Her dad stopped outside her favorite ice cream store and said, "So, what'll it be?"

Sophie loved ice cream as much as anything. Especially cookie dough ice cream. With hot fudge. And whipped cream. But ice cream was for kids who didn't take other kids' gifts. It was bad enough that she had taken a lollipop (even if it was brown). No way did she deserve ice cream. Or any other treat.

She looked down at the sidewalk. "I don't want anything, Dad."

"Mr. Charlie was right," her dad said. "You are not yourself today." He put his hand on her forehead. "Hmm. Feels okay to me. But let's go home and let your mom check."

Back at the car, Sophie climbed in. Her tote bag was still there. She tried hard not to think about it. But not hard enough.

Because Mia's gift was *all* she could think about, no matter what.

Sophie bet Mia had opened her other gifts by now. She was probably thinking, *Where's Kate's?*

In fact, she'd probably even called Kate to ask where it was. And Kate had probably said, "I don't know! Someone stole it, I think!"

And Mia had probably told her parents. And they'd probably checked all the pictures they'd taken. And they probably had one that showed Sophie by the table with the gifts. And another one, just after that, showing that Kate's gift had disappeared.

And by now, Mia was probably crying her eyes out. And her parents had probably called Sophie's house. And Sophie's mom had said, "She's not home yet." And Mia's parents had said, "She'll never get away with this. We're going to call the police —"

WEE-oo! WEE-oo! WEE-oo!

Wait! What was that?

WEE-OO! WEE-OO! WEE-OO!

It was a siren! And it was getting closer—fast!

Sophie was wrong. Mia's parents weren't thinking about calling the police.

Mia's parents *had* called the police!

Sophie could feel her dad pulling over. He probably thought they were stopping *him*, like on their trip to Washington, when he had driven a little too fast. She wondered what he would do when they said that *she* was the one under arrest.

He would be glad he hadn't bought her ice cream. That was for sure. He'd probably make her give back her root beer lollipop, too. Honestly? That was fine with her.

And then Sophie started to wonder: What would the police do with her? What were the consequences for doing dares? Would the judge be easy? Or tough?

After all, she had just done what Mindy had told her to do. Daredevils had to do things they didn't want to sometimes . . . right? Yes, of course.

But what if the judge didn't think so? What if they took her away?!

It was too horrible to think about. But Sophie couldn't stop.

"I'm sorry, Dad!" she cried out. The words jumped right out of her mouth. "I didn't mean to do anything bad! Don't let them put me in jail! Please!"

That was when the siren sound passed by them and faded away.

Sophie looked out the window to see a fire truck speeding down the street. It wasn't a police car after all!

Phew! She sighed. She was still free.

Then Sophie saw her dad's face. It was worried, and puzzled, and a few more things, all at once.

"What are you talking about, Sophie?" he asked.

Sophie looked at him and gulped.

CHAPTER 9

Where should she start? Sophie wasn't sure. So she just skipped to the end part.

"I have Mia's present. In my bag," Sophie told her dad.

Then she closed her eyes and waited. What would he say back?

But all he said was "Did you forget to give it to her?"

"No, Dad." He didn't understand. "It's not *my* present for her. It's Kate's," she said.

"Oh . . . So did *she* forget to give it to Mia?"

Sophie shook her head. "No, Dad." Then she took a deep breath. "I kind of . . . took it . . . from the gift table . . . at the party," she confessed.

Okay. *Now* her dad's forehead was wrinkling. He was getting it at last.

"Why did you take Mia's present?" he asked.

"Because Mindy VonBoffmann dared me to." Sophie's voice sounded very small. "And now that I'm a daredevil . . . I kind of . . . had to, Dad. You know?"

"You *had* to take Mia's present?" Her dad looked her straight in the eyes.

Sophie looked straight back at him. "Yeah," she said. "Didn't I?"

Her dad rubbed his chin for a minute. They were still stopped on the side of the road, so he turned the car off. He took off his glasses and cleaned them. That meant only one thing, Sophie knew. It was time to Have a Talk.

"Being a *daredevil*, Sophie—what exactly does it mean?" he asked.

Was that a trick question? Didn't everyone know?

"It means doing things that no one else would dare to do. No matter what they are."

"But don't you think there are sometimes good reasons why people don't do things?" her dad replied.

Sophie thought for a minute. "Do you mean because they're chicken?" she asked.

"No." Her dad shook his head. "I mean sometimes people don't do things because they know they're not *right*."

Oh.

"In fact, I always thought *you* were that kind of person," he went on.

"I am, Dad!" Sophie told him. Or at least . . . she used to be. She looked down at her tote bag. It was not the bag of someone who always did the right thing.

"I'm sorry, Dad." She sighed. "I made a big mistake."

He reached over and took her hand. "We all do. It's okay."

That made Sophie feel a little better. But she knew she had a long way to go. She'd never truly feel better until Mia had her present back. And she knew the longer she waited, the harder it would get.

"Dad?" She winced. It almost hurt to say what came next. "Do you think we could make one more stop on the way home?"

☆　☆　☆

Mia's house was outside of town, on the same big road as their school. Sophie didn't know the number of her house. She just knew that it was yellow. And there was a big basketball hoop in the driveway.

They drove by and she saw it. "That's it!" she yelled.

Her dad stomped on the brakes, made a U-turn, and pulled in.

Together, they walked to the front door. Sophie squeezed her dad's hand. He squeezed hers back, nice and hard. Then Sophie reached out and rang the bell.

Mia's mom answered the door. "Why, Sophie! Hi!" she said.

"Hi, Mrs. Carr." Sophie bit her lip. "Um . . . is Mia here?"

"Why, sure. She's in her room. Go on up," Mia's mom said. Then she turned to Sophie's dad. "We have a lot of leftover basketball cake. Would you like a piece?" she asked.

(So, it *was* a basketball cake. Sophie would have to tell that to Kate.)

The grown-ups went into the kitchen, and Sophie started up the stairs. She knew which room was Mia's—the first one on the right.

She poked her head in. "Mia?" She waved.

Mia's room wasn't super-girly. (Just like her. No big surprise.) The closest thing to a doll was a model skeleton on her dresser, next to a big fish tank.

Mia looked up. She was sitting on her bed with a pile of opened gifts on her right. On her left were neat rolls of ribbon and pieces of wrapping paper all folded up.

"Hi, Sophie! What are you doing here? Hey, I just opened your gift. Thanks a lot!"

She held up the present that Sophie had picked out herself.

"It's a friendship bracelet kit," said Sophie.

"I know! I love it!" Mia replied.

Then Mia held up a harmonica. And a big book about the stars. Plus a card game that Sophie liked a lot. And a puzzle that looked very hard.

"Wow. . . ," Sophie said when she found out all those gifts were from boys.

Mia also showed her a sparkly pink pillow. It was shaped like an *M*.

"It's from Mindy," Mia told her. Sophie could tell she thought it was *too* much.

Sophie kind of did, too. But she also kind of liked the sparkles (a lot!).

Sophie waited for Mia to tell her, "The only gift I don't have is Kate's. . . ." But Mia never did. So finally, Sophie brought it up herself.

"Did you know you had one more gift?" She reached into her bag and pulled out the silver gift. It was a little soggy from her towel.

"Wow, Sophie!" said Mia. "You didn't have to bring me another one. But thanks! That's really nice!"

Sophie shook her head and looked down. "No. It's really not," she said. "Because it's really not from me."

Mia's forehead crinkled. "Who's it from?"

Sophie sighed. "It's from Kate."

Mia made an I-don't-get-it face. So Sophie started to explain.

Of course, it wasn't easy. Explaining was almost as hard as taking the gift in the first place had been. But by the time she was done, she was happy that she did.

It felt good to give Mia her gift back. And something else felt good, too. When Sophie said, "I'm really sorry, Mia," Mia said, "It's okay. Besides, it was all *Mindy's* idea. Why do you think she'd make up such a mean dare?"

"I don't know," Sophie said. She really didn't have any idea. "It's like sometimes she just does things to make trouble between friends."

Mia rolled her eyes. "Does Mindy even know what a friend is?" Then she held up Kate's present. "Well, what are we waiting for? Let's open it!"

Sophie watched her untie the bow carefully and roll the ribbon up. Then Mia found where the paper was taped and used her fingernail to pry it off.

Sophie could hardly stand it. How could anyone be so slow?

At last, Mia peeled back the paper. Inside it was a box. And in the box was a small gum ball machine.

"Wow! This is cool!" said Mia.

"Yeah, it is!" Sophie had to agree.

Mia offered her a gum ball, and Sophie picked a red one. But before they could try out one of Mia's new games, it was time for Sophie to go.

"Sophie, I'm really proud of you," her dad said as he drove her home.

"You are?" Sophie leaned forward. She was surprised to hear that. "Even after I did Mindy's dare?" she asked.

"Well, no. I'm not proud of you for doing *that*," he said. "But I am proud of you for making it right. And for doing it all on your own."

Sophie smiled. Yeah. Come to think of it, she felt pretty proud of herself, too.

CHAPTER 10

Sophie was still feeling proud — and daring — on Monday morning, when she walked into room 10.

That was why she was so happy to see Mindy. She walked up to her at the coatrack.

"Good morning, Mindy," she said with a grin.

Mindy turned. She was grinning, too — at first. But then her grin started to fade, and Sophie was pretty sure she knew why. It was because Sophie was holding hands with Mia and Kate.

The three of them looked at Mindy. And Mindy looked back.

"I thought . . . ," Mindy started. But then she stopped. Her lips were pinched.

Sophie nodded. "I know." She helped Mindy finish: "You thought Mia and Kate would be mad at me for doing that dare. But I just wanted you to know that everything worked out okay. I took the gift to Mia later. And then I went and told Kate the whole story."

Mindy's mouth fell open. But nothing at all came out.

That was when Lily ran up, breathless. "Sorry I'm late, Mindy," she gasped. "Did you have to hang your coat up all by yourself? I just couldn't find my headband *anywhere*. Hey, what did I miss?"

Kate and Mia put their arms around Sophie. "Oh, nothing," they said. Then they all walked away together. Sophie had to say, it was pretty great to have good friends!

"I'm glad you told me everything this weekend, Sophie," Kate said.

Then Mia reached into her pocket. She pulled out two colorful braids. They were friendship bracelets she'd made that weekend — and there was one for each of them. Mia helped them tie them on. Sophie loved hers. It was purple and green.

Eve ran up. "Hey, Sophie. Are you still doing dares?"

Sophie nodded. "Yeah." Then she held up a finger. "But now I do have *rules*."

Eve giggled. "Okay. Well, guess what. Sydney has one for you." She waved and called Sydney over. "Hey, Sydney. Tell Sophie your dare!"

Hang on.

Something about the way their eyes shone made Sophie put up her hand. "My rule is I'll do any dare unless it *hurts* someone," she said.

"Oh, this won't hurt," Sydney assured her.

"Okay, then." Sophie took a deep breath. She stood up very straight and tall.

Sydney snickered. Eve did, too.

"I dare you to kiss Toby Myers!" Sydney said.

Kiss? Toby Myers?!

Sophie looked around for a place to throw up.

"Well?" Sydney tried to ask, but she was laughing too hard by then.

Sophie didn't even have to think. Her answer came out fast. "Forget it. I quit. I'm done. I am not a daredevil anymore," she announced.

Eve looked disappointed. Kate and Mia laughed, but they looked a little disappointed, too.

But Sydney looked happy. "Hey, I found a dare you couldn't do!"

Sydney was *very* happy after that. And Sophie supposed she was, too. She was glad she didn't have to do things she didn't want to do anymore. But she missed that tingly feeling she got from the good dares. And she missed being special. Being Sophie the Nothing again was hard.

She was thinking about that later as she walked out to the bus. And that was when

Sophie saw Ms. Moffly walking out, too, carrying a big box.

Ms. Moffly's face looked like the box was heavy. Sophie knew what that was like. Sometimes her mom made Sophie help her carry groceries from the car. And sometimes Sophie got the milk *and* the orange juice in one bag. Talk about heavy! That could break off an arm.

Sophie ran up to Ms. Moffly. She put her hands under the box. "Can I help you, Ms. Moffly?"

"Oh, thank you, Sophie," Ms. Moffly panted. "You're such a sweetheart!"

A sweetheart...

Sophie the Sweetheart?

Sophie wasn't sure if she was glowing. But she kind of thought she was!

She started to say, "You're welcome. I *am* a sweetheart. How did you know?" But before she could, two more hands reached for the box. Sophie looked up. They were Mr. Bloom's.

Mr. Bloom was another teacher (a teacher who wore jeans and no tie). He taught Hayley's fifth-grade class. And he rode to school on a bike, like a kid.

He had his helmet on now, in fact. So Sophie couldn't see much of his hair. But she could see the deep dimples on each side of his big grin.

"Here, Lila. Let me help you," he said.

"Oh, thank you," Ms. Moffly said back.

Sophie wondered if she would call him a sweetheart, too.

She held her breath and waited . . . but Ms. Moffly didn't. Sophie sighed, relieved. She wanted to be the *only* sweetheart around.

Or wait . . . did she?

Maybe not!

Maybe it *would* be nice if Ms. Moffly called Mr. Bloom sweetheart—in a different kind of way.

And maybe Sophie the Sweetheart could help that happen. . . .

How sweet would that be?

Sophie's new name is
going to be super-sweet!

Take a peek at Sophie's next adventure....

Dear Ms. Moffly,
   I love you.
   Will you marry me?
   Sinseerly, Mr. Bloom

There. Sophie put down her pen. *That should work!* She grinned. Then she turned to her best friend, Kate Barry. Did she agree?

It was all part of their big plan. A plan they'd just made that afternoon in Sophie's room. A plan to get their third-grade teacher, Ms. Moffly, to marry the fifth-grade teacher, Mr. Bloom.

At first, Kate had thought it was a little crazy. "Ms. Moffly? And Mr. Bloom? Doesn't he wear *jeans*? I don't think Ms. Moffly even has those."

Then Sophie explained how much the two

had in common: "They both teach at Ordinary Elementary School!"

And she explained how cool it would be if they got married: "That means a wedding! And of course that means we get to go!"

"Oh!" That made Kate's eyebrows bounce. Then she thought of something, too. "Hey! Know what else that means?"

"What?"

"It means a honeymoon!"

Sophie nodded. "You're right! Do you think we'd get to go on that, too?"

"Probably not." Kate giggled and rolled her eyes. "But it might mean no school."

Oh. Well, that was almost as good. It fact, it was pretty great. But not as great as the other thing Sophie was hoping for: an awesome, perfect name!

Sophie was tired—*exhausted* even—of being Sophie the Most Average Girl in the Whole School. And she was determined to start being Sophie the...Anything Else. Just something that made her stand out from the rest of the world.

And now she had the best idea! She had gotten it at the end of school that day. Ms. Moffly had been struggling with a box, and Sophie had run up to help.

"Sophie, you're such a sweetheart," Ms. Moffly had told her.

And that was it!

Sophie the Sweetheart! Who could ask for a better name than that? All she had to do was keep being sweet and helpful to Ms. Moffly. And everybody else.

Sophie figured it wouldn't be too hard. At least not as hard as living up to some other names had been. She was pretty good at being sweet, really. She just forgot now and then. But this time she would remember, every second of every day. And what could possibly be sweeter than helping Ms. Moffly get a sweetheart of her own?

"So do you think it's enough?" Sophie asked Kate. She held the letter up for both of them to read.

Kate nodded. "Yeah, it sounds good." Then she frowned. "But what about the handwriting?"

Huh? Sophie studied the page. "I tried to be so neat. And look, there's a heart above the 'i.'"

She could have written it in cursive, she guessed. But those *f*'s were so hard to make!

"I think it might be *too* neat," Kate said. "Grown-up writing never looks as neat as that."

Oh . . . right. Sophie thought about her mom's handwriting. That was a mess.

"Okay." She reached for a clean sheet of paper. "Let me try again."

"Hang on. There's something else," Kate said.

Sophie's pen froze.

Kate went on. "I wonder if we should use first names. Like maybe say 'Dear Lila,' instead."

"Good idea!" said Sophie. Why hadn't she thought of that?

"'Dear *Lila*...'" She started writing. Then she stopped. "Uh-oh. Do you know what Mr. Bloom's first name is?" she asked Kate.

Kate did not. Too bad.

But someone else does! Sophie remembered when that someone walked in right then.

"Hayley!"

Sophie's big sister just happened to be in Mr. Bloom's class. Sophie waved her pen as her sister brushed past her bed. "I have a very important question for you!" she said.

Hayley kept walking toward her dresser. "No, I will *not* play Monopoly with you," she said. "You guys always gang up against me, and anyway, I'm way too busy right now. I have to change for ballet."

Sophie sighed. She wished that just once Hayley would remember this was her room, too. But she wasn't going to let that bother her. At least, not so much.

"Don't worry. That's not my question," Sophie

messier, yes. But I'm not talking about that. I'm talking about what happens when Ms. Moffly says, 'Yes.' And Mr. Bloom says 'Huh?' because he doesn't even know he asked."

Oh.

Sophie nodded. "I see," she said, thinking hard. "So do you think the note should be from Ms. Moffly, instead?"

"No." Hayley shook her head again. "Besides, don't you read or watch TV? People go on *dates* first. They don't just get married."

"They don't?" Sophie frowned. She thought that was exactly what they did.

"No." Hayley rolled her eyes. "You'll know that when you're ten."

Sophie turned to Kate. She could tell this was news to her, too. But if Ms. Moffly and Mr. Bloom had to go out on a *date* first, then that's what they would do.

Sophie slapped the paper down on her lap desk. Then she took her pen and went back to work.

Dear ~~Ms. Moffty,~~ Lila,
I love you.
Will you ~~marry me?~~ Go on a date with me?
Sinseerly, ~~Mr. Bloom~~ Mike
P.S. Then will you marry me?

When she was done, Sophie showed it to Hayley. "Better?" she asked.

Hayley shrugged. But she didn't look so sure.

WHERE EVERY PUPPY FINDS A HOME

KITTY CORNER

Where kitties get the love they need

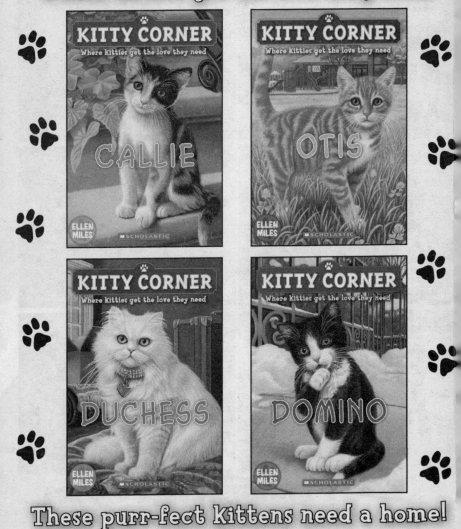

These purr-fect kittens need a home!

SCHOLASTIC